THE MYSTERY IN

Chocolate Town

HERSHEY, PENNSYLVANIA

First Edition ©2007 Carole Marsh/Gallopade International/Peachtree City, GA
Current Edition ©January 2015
Ebook Edition ©2011
All rights reserved.
Manufactured in Peachtree City, GA

Carole Marsh Mysteries™ and its skull colophon are the property of Carole Marsh and Gallopade International.

Published by Gallopade International/Carole Marsh Books. Printed in the United States of America.

Managing Editor: Sherry Moss
Cover Design: Vicki DeJoy
Picture Credits: Allison Fortune, Carole Marsh
Content Design: Joyce Revoir Illustration & Design, Inc.

A special thanks to Pamela Whitenack and Tammy Hamilton of The Hershey Community Archives.

HERSHEY'S, HERSHEY'S KISSES, CHOCOLATE WORLD, CHOCOLATE TOWN, AND HERSHEY THE SWEETEST PLACE ON EARTH are registered trademarks of the Hershey Chocolate & Confectionary Corporation.

Gallopade International is introducing SAT words that kids need to know in each new book that we publish. The SAT words are bold in the story. Look for this special logo beside each word in the glossary. Happy Learning!

Gallopade is proud to be a member and supporter of these educational organizations and associations:

American Booksellers Association
American Library Association
International Reading Association
National Association for Gifted Children
The National School Supply and Equipment Association
The National Council for the Social Studies
Museum Store Association
Association of Partners for Public Lands
Association of Booksellers for Children
Association for the Study of African American Life and History
National Alliance of Black School Educators

Once upon a time...

Hmm, kids keep asking me to write a mystery book. What shall I do?

Mimi

Write one about spiders!

Papa said …

Why don't you set the stories in real locations?

That's a great idea! And if I do that, I might as well choose real kids as characters in the stories! But which kids would I pick?

MIMI, PICK ME, PICK ME!

ME, TOO, MIMI, PICK ME, TOO!

Christina

Grant

Pick me!

On the *Mystery Girl* airplane ...

I can FLY us anywhere!

Mystery Girl

Or aboard the *Mimi!*

Mimi

Take me to the Forbidden City!

Or by surfboard, rickshaw, motorbike, camel ...

All great ideas! I can put a lot of history, **MYSTERY,** legend, lore, and **laughs** in the books! We can use other boys and girls in the books. It will be educational and fun!

Good stuff!

The *Mystery Girl* is all revved up—let's go!

You mean now?

LET'S GO!

And so, Mimi, Papa, Christina, and Grant took off aboard the *Mystery Girl* and America's National Mystery Book Series—where the adventure is real and so are the characters! —was born.

START YOUR ADVENTURE TODAY!

READ THE BOOK!

GO ONLINE!

TRACK YOUR ADVENTURES!

APPLY TO BE A CHARACTER!

Yikes! That was close!

Rats!

10

1

I SMELL CHOCOLATE

"I smell chocolate," Grant mumbled, half asleep in the back of the SUV Papa had rented at the airport. Just an hour earlier, they had landed in Papa's little red and white airplane, the *Mystery Girl*, at the airport in Harrisburg, Pennsylvania.

"No, you don't, Grant," his sister, Christina, grumbled. "It's just your imagination, silly."

It was almost midnight and everyone— including their grandparents, Mimi and Papa—were sleepy. It had been a long day and a long flight; fog had caused delays. Usually when the foursome embarked on one of their travel adventures, they all were noisy and rowdy and teasing and laughing; that was part of the fun of traveling with their grandparents, who acted more like fourth-graders than old fogeys.

But tonight was different. They'd missed dinner. "I want to get to the hotel," Papa insisted. "We can eat then." But the foggy roads had caused them to creep along for the last hour.

Mimi snored softly in the front seat. Papa sang "Good Night, Irene" over and over under his breath. Christina figured he was trying to stay awake. It had been a workday for him and Mimi, who was a children's mystery book writer. Papa was her "wrangler, travel agent, cowboy, pilot, trail boss, and chief factotum," as he always put it. This always made Mimi giggle and her blue eyes beam.

"I really, really do smell chocolate," Grant insisted yet again.

Christina tugged on the blanket she and her brother were unsuccessfully trying to share in the backseat. It was February and it was cold; real cold. The back windows were blurred with frost.

"You really, really don't smell chocolate," Christina said. She was 10 and Grant was only 7, so she usually got the last word in most things—but not this time.

For suddenly, Mimi roared to life in the front seat. First, her curly blond hair popped up over the seat, then the arms of her red suit began to flail as she wiped at her window with a tissue.

"I SMELL CHOCOLATE!" Mimi hollered. Mimi was an admitted "chocoholic." She loved all things chocolate.

Just as Christina prepared to argue with her grandmother, she suddenly had the strangest sensation. "Ohmigosh!" she said. "I smell chocolate, too!"

"Told ya!" said Grant, with a yawn. He rolled over, pulling the blanket entirely off his sister.

"EXCUSE ME!" cried Papa. "EXCUSE ME! Do any of you even remember where we're going on this trip? I know we started out what seems like ages ago, but actually it was only this afternoon after school and work. But we were headed somewhere—remember?"

At the same time, Christina and Grant tugged two corners of the blanket and wiped swirly circles on their windows.

"Wow! Look at that!" said Grant, in a dreamy voice. "Streetlights...streetlights that look exactly like Hershey Kisses."

His sister laughed. "They *are* Hershey Kisses, Grant. Now, I remember, Papa. We're going to Hershey, Pennsylvania, the Sweetest Place on Earth!"

"Uh, we're not going there," said Papa. "We're actually here!"

The creepy fog cleared just enough for them to see that they had stopped in front of the Hotel Hershey.

"Thank goodness," said Mimi, quickly combing her hair and fixing her lipstick. A bellman headed out of the fog to help them with their luggage. Mimi always had a lot of luggage. She didn't go anywhere without her red suits, high heels, laptop computer, research books, camera, a fancy ball gown, and Papa's tuxedo (which he called his "penguin suit"). Mimi always said you just never knew when you might be invited to a black-tie ball. She and Papa loved to dance.

"This place looks mysterious in the fog," Christina told her grandmother. Mimi was here to do research for a mystery she planned to set in the world-famous town of chocolate: Hershey, Pennsylvania.

"Oh, I doubt there's anything mysterious about a town devoted to candy and kids and fun," said Mimi.

"Don't be so sure," said Papa, getting out of the car with a yawn and a stretch. He wore his usual outfit of dress jeans, black leather vest, bolo, cowboy boots, and Stetson hat. He pushed the button to unlock the back gate for the bellman. "Mystery seems to follow you around, woman!" Mimi laughed.

"Oh, maybe I'll just write a little cozy this time," she said.

"What's that?" asked Christina, gathering her backpack and jacket.

Mimi slipped on her coat as Papa opened the door for her. "It's just a quiet, little old-lady kind of mystery where people sit around and drink tea."

"I don't think kids will like that," argued Grant. He wadded the blanket up under his arm and inhaled deeply, as if he could make the scent of chocolate rush down to his growling tummy.

"Why not?" said Mimi.

"Whatever the mystery is, I think kids will want the characters to drink hot chocolate, not tea," answered Grant.

"I agree!" said Christina.

Papa laughed as he hustled them toward the foggy-windowed hotel. It was spitting snow. "You know, you kids are characters in Mimi's books," he reminded them.

Christina and Grant just looked at one another and shook their heads. "That's what we mean, Papa!" said Christina. "We want to drink some hot chocolate!"

"And soooooooon," groaned Grant, rubbing his tummy. "And maybe eat some chocolate candy bars and chocolate pie and..."

Just then the bellman opened the doors to the hotel's Fountain Lobby and the kids staggered inside. For a moment, they were speechless. Mimi and Papa just smiled.

"Well, if we want chocolate," Christina finally squeaked... "I think we've come to the RIGHT PLACE!"

2
THE RIGHT PLACE

The **opulent** lobby mesmerized Christina and Grant. They plopped their backpacks and jackets on the beautiful mosaic tile floor and craned their necks to stare up at the sky blue ceiling with clouds painted on it. A large fountain spurted in the center of the room. Palm trees scattered around the lobby added to the exotic, even sort of spooky, feeling.

"Wow!" said Christina. "I didn't know we were going to stay in a palace, Mimi."

Even though she was exhausted, Mimi laughed. "More like an Italian villa," she said. "The Hershey is an historic hotel, you know. It dates back to the 1930s."

Just then, Papa called for Mimi to join him at the registration desk. He looked aggravated.

Grant, who had wandered off to look around, dashed back to Christina, scooting along on the marble floor on his Heelies. "Hey, Christina," he whispered loudly.

"I can hear you!" his sister said. "Everyone can hear you."

Grant looked all around. He shrugged his shoulders. "But there's no one here...except us chickens, as Papa always says."

His sister groaned. "They why are you whispering?" She knew they were all so tired and hungry that they were getting cranky. She could hear Papa's voice getting louder at the registration desk; there must be a problem, she thought.

Her brother had scooted off toward a group of palm trees near the fountain. "Pssst!" he hissed back toward Christina. When she ignored him, he repeated "PSSSSSSST!" so loudly that even the bellman looked up. But not, Christina noted, the two security guards huddled in conversation behind the palms.

Quickly, Christina sidled up to her brother. "What gives?"

"I don't know," Grant whispered, very quietly this time. "I'm eavesdropping. These two guys are talking about a big deal theft—right here in Hershey, just earlier tonight, as nearly as I can tell."

"Whoa," said Christina. "Trouble in Paradise...I like it!" She was fond of mysteries, puzzles, riddles, intrigue, spies, spying, and anything like that. Mimi always said she had inherited her mystery genes and maybe she would grow up to be a writer one day. Christina hoped so.

"It's silver dollars!" Grant said. "I wish they'd talk louder."

Suddenly, the security guards looked over at the two children. They gave them a fake smile, then quietly moved to the other side of the fountain where they continued their conversation out of earshot of the nosy kids.

"Over here!" Papa called. He was smiling now.

As the kids approached the registration desk, Mimi said, "There was some confusion about our reservation, but now we're all squared away. We're going to have lovely adjoining suites."

Christina giggled. Mimi always loved it when they got upgraded to a swankier room. She knew Papa was a good finagler when it came to arranging such things. And she and her brother loved separate rooms—it was so much easier to sneak out and explore, when necessary. And for she and Grant, it was always necessary!

The beaming desk clerk handed Papa the keys. In a bright, chirpy voice she said "WELCOME TO THE SWEETEST PLACE ON EARTH!"

Grant grinned and whispered to Christina. "If we're lucky, maybe not as sweet as they think?"

Christina grinned back. "Fog, chocolate, and mystery afoot—what more could we want?"

Her brother groaned and rubbed his tummy. "Something to eat," he begged. "Pleeeeaaasse? And make mine chocolate!"

3
MYSTERY AFOOT?

As Mimi steered them toward the elevator, Grant balked. "Really, I'm serious. Aren't we going to eat? My bellybutton's kissing my backbone." He moaned and doubled over.

The bellman laughed as he lurched the luggage cart onto the elevator. "Don't worry, young man," he said. "I'm sorry all our restaurants are closed, but I think you'll find an acceptable midnight snack in your rooms."

"Is it midnight?" Christina asked. She loved to stay up past midnight, especially on New Year's Eve to hear the church bells ringing and fireworks popping in the distance.

Papa looked at his watch. "Oh, yes," he said. "It's past midnight—the witching hour."

"Ohh," said Grant. "What does that mean?"

His grandfather yawned. "It means that I'm sure witching I could go to bed right now!"

As soon as they entered their suite, and began to "ooh" and "aah" at the luxurious rooms, Papa said, "Goodnight, Irenes!" and headed into one of the bedrooms and closed the door.

The bellman deposited their luggage. Mimi tipped him, and he left with a short bow and a doff of his cap.

By that time, Christina and Grant had gone through the connecting doorway to their room. When Mimi joined them, she found her two grandchildren standing there with their mouths hanging open. "What's wrong?" she asked.

Together, the two kids pointed at the basket sitting on the dresser. It was enormous, and was filled with heaping piles of fruit and chocolate—Hershey Bars, Kit Kat Bars, York Peppermint Patties, and Hershey's Kisses galore— so many they even spilled out of the basket and all around the top of the dresser.

Mimi laughed. "Dig in!" she ordered. "And while you snack, get your pajamas on. I'm going to take a quick shower."

Before their grandmother could leave the room, the two hungry kids dashed for the basket.

Together they hauled it over to one of the twin beds and dumped it out onto the bedspread.

"Wow!" said Grant. "Look at all this stuff! This is better than Halloween. Better than trick-or-treat, better than...mrgfhgrr pfgsghrlw!"

His sister could no longer understand her brother because his mouth was now filled with a big wad of chocolate. She chose a banana and Grant looked at her like she was crazy. Christina shrugged. "I'm just too tired," she confessed.

"Grant!" Mimi called from the bathroom. "Would you go down the hall and get some ice, please. Papa would like some water."

"Surembghret, Mimi!" Grant called back. He swallowed hard and grinned. "That's better," he said, wiping a GOT CHOCOLATE rim from his lips. "Ahhhhh." He hopped off the bed and scampered to the door.

Christina finished her banana and put on her pajamas. She unpacked her backpack, and then to help her brother, she unpacked his backpack and put his pajamas on his bed. When he didn't come back, she began to get worried. She went into the living room that connected the adjoining bedrooms. From there she could hear Papa snoring softly. She could hear the water running in the shower in the bathroom. So, she opened the door to the hall and peeked outside.

She looked up and down the hallway. It was quiet as a tomb. She was a little worried; what could be taking her brother so long, she wondered. Suddenly, she spotted something far down the hall, just a shadow she thought. But when she squinted hard, she could see it was Grant. He was squatting down in front of a room, and it looked like he was peeking in a keyhole!

"Grant!" she called in as quiet a loud whisper as she could muster. When he did not look her way, she repeated a little more loudly, "GRANT!"

From back inside their room, she heard her grandmother call, "Grant, are you back yet?"

On an impulse, Christina stepped out into the hall. "Grant," she hissed one last time. "You'd better come on, now, can you hear me? Mimi's calling!"

Grant still didn't look up. Exasperated, Christina took another step further down the hall and put her hands on her hips. When she did, she heard an awful sound: the sound of the door closing behind her. And she and Grant had no key. In a huff, she tugged her pajama bottoms up a little and marched down the hall.

As she got closer to Grant and was just about to start to fuss at him, her brother looked up at her with big, scared eyes. Slowly, but insistently, he shook his head back and forth. "NO!" he mouthed silently. Then, with the tip of his finger, he beckoned her to come closer.

With goose bumps prickling her arms, Christina tiptoed down the hall toward the dark corner where her brother seemed frozen in place.

26

4
FOREVER EAVESDROPPING

"Grant, what are you doing?" Christina whispered as soon as she joined her brother. He just pulled her down by her pajama sleeve.

"Eavesdropping, what else?" he whispered back. Beside him sat the filled ice bucket. Melting ice dripped water over the edge and onto the carpet.

"Well, stop!" Christina insisted. "It's not polite to eavesdrop."

"But we do it all the time," Grant argued. "We're forever eavesdropping."

Christina sighed. It was true. It did seem like when you went on mystery adventures, you were forever eavesdropping to try to learn some new information. Adults could do things "by the book," but kids had to be inventive to solve a mystery, she thought. Sometimes, it was pretty exhausting!

"But, Grant," she said. "It's way past midnight. Who's still up at this hour anyway?"

Her brother grinned. He nodded toward the keyhole. In spite of herself, Christina took a peek. She was flabbergasted at what she saw!

Now she looked at her brother with the same wide-eyed stare that he had given her just a moment ago. Neither of them could believe what they were seeing.

"It's those same two security guards," Grant said.

Christina peeked again. "I think you're right," she said. "But what's all that on the table?"

"Well, duh," said her brother. "Money, what else, and lots of it!"

Once more Christina stared through the keyhole. Sure enough, there was a heaping pile of money on the table–all silver dollars! It looked like pirate treasure, or something out of a fairy tale.

"But why are they doing what they're doing?" she asked her brother.

Grant shook his head. "I have no idea why they would be wrapping each silver dollar in foil paper," he said. "But they've been doing it the whole time I've been looking. It will take them all night."

Just then, they heard a gruff voice way down the hall: PAPA!

"Come, on, Grant!" insisted Christina.

Her brother jumped up, knocking the ice bucket over with a clatter. From inside the room, they could hear the two men jump up out of their chairs, and a few of the coins jangle as they spilled to the floor.

"Hurry!" Christina urged, making a mad dash down the hall.

Grant grabbed the half-empty ice bucket and ran after his sister.

When he glanced back, he saw a man stick his head out of the doorway to the room. He glared at the kids and shook his fist, then slammed the door.

When they reached their room, Mimi was standing there holding the door open with a scowl on her face. "Hmm," she said, as she took the ice bucket Grant handed her. She looked at her grandchildren suspiciously. "Ice shortage...in February?" she asked.

Neither kid answered. Both just gave their grandmother a sweet, innocent smile and said, "Goodnight!" as they vanished into their room, turned the light off, and jumped into bed.

The next morning, it wasn't mystery afoot, it was snow afoot—in fact, about a foot of it!

"WOOOOOOW!" squealed Grant, the first to wake up and look out the hotel window.

"SUPER!" shouted Christina. She loved snow. They seldom got any back in their home state of Georgia. Mostly they got a messy "wintry mix," which was no fun at all.

"YEE-HA!" said Papa, when he viewed the freshly-frosted outdoors. He had been born in western Iowa and adored snow. His grandchildren loved to hear him tell old-timey tales of sledding, snowball fights, and ice skating all over town when the streets froze over.

Even Mimi was delighted. "What tastes better than cocoa in the snow!" she said. "I can get some great pictures today."

Soon, the room service waiter delivered breakfast on large silver trays: bacon, eggs, toast, hot chocolate, and, of course, Hershey's Kisses.

"Boy, howdy, this is the cat's pajamas," said Grant. "Breakfast with dessert!"

Christina tried to spread her toast with a Kiss. "Cats don't wear pajamas," she reminded her brother.

"Speaking of pajamas," said Mimi, sweetly. "Why were you wandering around the hall last night, young lady, in yours?" She pointed her butter knife Christina's way.

Papa looked up from his newspaper. No matter where he was, he always had to read the newspaper every day. "You gotta keep up with what's going on the in the world," he always said. But right now, he said, "Huh? You mean I take a little nap before bedtime and you kids parade around outside in your PJ's?"

"Not me," said Grant. "I had on my clothes." When his grandparents stared at him, he said, "Oops!" and blushed.

"Nothing like confessing to the crime," Christina groused. "Grant just went to get ice," she explained to her grandfather. "Mimi told him to. I just went to find him."

Mimi buttered her toast and topped it with orange marmalade. "Yes, he brought back six whole ice cubes," she reminded them. "This is the sweetest place on earth," their grandmother reminded them. "And I want you to be sweet while we're here."

"And stay out of trouble, you hooligan ragamuffins, too!" teased Papa.

Their grandmother groaned. "I'm serious," Mimi said. "We're here on official mystery writing business and do not want to embarrass ourselves. No mystery shenanigans. Research first; mystery writing when I get back home. I don't need your help this time—puhleeeeeese."

"Did you say police?" asked Grant with a giggle.

"I said PLEASE!" Mimi said, tossing a pillow Grant's way.

And the next thing you knew, the entire family was enjoying a first class pillow fight! The lovely goose down pillows were perfect for it, except for the few feathers it left floating in the cocoa.

Just then the doorbell to their suite rang. Dodging a flying pillow, Papa opened the door. There stood a very serious-looking woman. Grant thought she looked like a librarian. Christina thought she looked like a school principal. She gave them all the look of a disapproving nanny as she said, "The mystery-writing family, I suppose?"

Trying hard to look proper, Mimi laid down her pillow and brushed a feather from her hair. "And you are?" she asked sweetly, raising an eyebrow.

The woman nodded. "And I am Emmalou Liberty. I am your Hershey guide for the day."

Papa choked on his toast. "Uh, I don't think we need a guide; I think we need a sled."

"Then I shall provide one," the woman said. She turned on her heels and left.

As soon as Papa closed the door, they all broke out into laughter. Papa mocked the woman by standing tall and bowing and pursing his lips: "I AM YOUR GUIDE; FOLLOW ME!"

Grant and Christina howled, but Mimi shushed them. "Stop now, be nice. I think it's great that someone provided us with our own private concierge for the day." She headed off to get dressed.

"But who did?" asked Christina. "You didn't mention a guide."

Mimi turned. "Well, I have no idea. I guess I just forgot. Maybe the town of Hershey is just trying to be the sweetest place on earth to us; let's enjoy that. It will be a help. We've never been here before, you know."

Grant put on a serious scowl. "So she's a stranger—very suspicious...verrrrrry suspicious." He did his silly imitation of a Sherlock Holmes-type detective, marching around the room with his hands behind his back, looking under the pillows and plates, as if searching for clues.

His grandmother giggled. "Don't even start with me, Grant," she warned. "Go put some warm clothes on."

"So we can go sledding?" Grant said with a grin.

"No!" said Mimi. "So we can go researching. It's a workday."

"Awwww," said Christina, falling back onto a pile of pillows. "We might as well have stayed in school."

Suddenly, there was a TAP SPLAT PLOP on the window. When the kids ran and pulled back the curtains, they saw Emmalou Liberty down below. She had thrown snowballs at their window. She was not smiling. But she was holding four bright orange toboggans!

5
A SLEDDING WE WILL GO!

"Cool!" squealed Grant. "Let's go!" He tossed one last pillow at his sister, but she was moving so fast to the bedroom to get dressed that he missed her completely.

"Hey," said Mimi, "what about work?"

Papa just gave her a look. "Just a short after-breakfast jaunt?" He was already pulling on his long underwear.

Mimi grinned. "Why not?!" she said, and suddenly the entire suite was in a flurry of commotion as hats, mittens, and boots went a-flying until finally everyone was dressed and ready to head downstairs.

"But what about the mystery?" Christina asked her brother, as they hurried toward the elevator.

"Aw, I imagine those guys are still in their room wrapping all those silver dollars in foil. We'll catch up with them later and foil their plans—whatever their plans are," said Grant.

"Very funny, Grant," said his sister. But the next thing she knew, Papa had whisked them all outdoors where Emmalou Liberty was waiting with the sleds.

For at least an hour, the family had a blast sliding down the big hill below the Hotel Hershey. The snow was soft and fluffy, so tumbling off your toboggan was just as much fun as staying on it. A few of the other hotel guests were sledding too, and everyone was laughing.

Finally, Mimi, Papa, and the other adults called it quits and headed for the café to get something warm to drink. Only Christina, Grant, and another boy and girl were left outdoors.

"Hi," Christina said to the girl. "Are you visiting Hershey, too?"

The girl, named Annabelle, brushed her long, blond hair out of her face. "Not really," she said. "I'm just here for a couple of days with my dad. He sells chocolate-making products to the Hershey factory. My school's on winter break, so I got to come along with him."

"Us, too," said Christina. "Winter break I mean. It was lucky for us they had snow."

"Very!" agreed a boy who joined them. "I'm Sean...S E A N, but you pronounce it Shawn. Can I sled with you guys?"

"Sure," said Christina, looking at Annabelle. "Okay with you?"

Annabelle nodded as Grant suddenly swooshed down the hill toward them. The kids had to jump out of his way so as not to be bowled over like bowling balls!

"Whoa, little buddy!" cried Sean. "Take it easy there, will ya?"

Christina gave Sean a funny look. "Uh, I don't think Grant will like being called 'little buddy,' Sean. He is my little brother, but he doesn't like that 'little' part rubbed in his face."

Sean nodded. "Right. Got it. I remember those days." He reached down and grabbed Grant by the hand to help him up, but Grant just rolled over on his back and started making snow angels.

"Now he's showing off," Christina explained.

Annabelle laughed. "Aw, he's just having fun." She plopped down and started swinging her arms and legs just like Grant.

With a thud, Sean plopped down too and did the same thing.

"If you can't beat em, join em," said Christina. She laid down in the snow and flailed her arms and legs in a windmill pattern. It was snowing again. She closed her eyes and felt the cool flakes collect on her eyelashes. When she opened her eyes, the other three kids were standing up staring down at her. "You tricked me!" she said, laughing.

"It was your brother's idea," said Sean, patting Grant on the head.

"I can see we're all going to get along fine," said Annabelle. "I was hoping to find some friends to play with. Dad's going to be in meetings all day. I was just going to mope around my room and do homework."

"My mom's over at the convention center teaching a seminar on business," said Sean. "I'm hanging out by myself, too."

"Well, now we're all hanging out together!" cheered Grant loudly.

Annabelle rubbed her red nose. "I don't know about you guys, but I'm getting cold. Can we go inside and have some cocoa?"

Sean rubbed his chin with his gloved hand.

"Hmm," he said. "I wonder if they have any hot chocolate around this place?"

The other kids laughed. Annabelle swiped up a handful of snow and tossed it at Sean.

"What else is there to do around this place?" said Sean, as they trudged up the snowy hill, tugging their toboggans behind them.

Christina looked at Grant. Grant looked at Christina. Together they said, "How about solving a real life mystery?!"

6
ALL IN!

When they got to the hotel, they were greeted in the lobby by Mimi, all dressed in her red suit, ready to do "mystery writing business."

Grant and Christina introduced their new friends. "Can't we please have some hot chocolate with them?" begged Christina.

Mimi tapped the toe of her red shoe. "Well, okay. Papa's gone to get the car. So have something warm to drink and then meet us here. We have to get to the Hershey Museum."

When the kids heard the word museum, they groaned. They really liked museums, but not on a snowy winter day when they had just met new friends and had a mystery to solve.

Suddenly, Christina had a brainstorm. "Would it be okay if our new friends came to the museum with us?" she asked her grandmother. "Their parents are busy on business too. They were just going to stay in their rooms." Christina put on her most authentic "isn't that just awful and boring" face.

Mimi took the bait. "Well, alright," she said. She smiled at Annabelle and Sean. "As long as they get permission from their parents. But gulp down that cocoa and get back here in five minutes—promise?"

"Promise!" shouted all the kids together.

Mimi just shook her head and walked off, cell phone in hand, to make some calls. The kids scampered toward the café.

"So, what mystery?!" Sean asked, as soon as they found a table and sat down.

Christina and Grant recounted the strange events from the night before. It all seemed very peculiar to Annabelle. She seemed quite **skeptical**. "You guys must really have a big imagination. Maybe those men were just playing cards, or wrapping candy, or..." She did not finish her sentence.

Grant frowned, but he waited until their waitress put down their mugs of cocoa before he spoke. "Or what?" he asked. "I saw what I saw. My sister and I are mystery experts; we know one when we see one, girlie!"

Christina giggled. "Take it easy, Grant," she warned her brother. "It does sound pretty preposterous. Even I was shocked when I looked through the keyhole." She noticed that Sean was being very quiet and had a funny look on his face. "What?" she demanded. "What?!"

Without a word, Sean got up and went over to a table in the café. He grabbed a daily newspaper and came back. He laid it down on the table so they all could read the front page headline: THIEVES STEAL ELDERLY HERSHEY MAN'S 900 SILVER DOLLAR FORTUNE!

It took a minute for it to sink in. Finally, Christina said, "Oh, my goodness. So that's the pile of silver dollars we saw last night?"

Sean shrugged. "Seems so."

"Well I never!" declared Annabelle.

"Never what?" asked Grant.

Annabelle giggled. "Grant, you're funny!"

Grant sat up very straight and beamed. "Yeah, everybody tells me that; guess it's just my job."

Christina frowned. "You know, Mimi will be looking for a mystery for her new book," she said. "Usually she just makes one up. But this real-life mystery could be really cool."

Sean gulped down his cocoa. "Only one problem," he said.

"What?" asked Christina, sipping on her chocolate.

"The mystery's gotta be solved!" he said.

Grant waved his hand in the air as if he were in class asking permission to go to the bathroom. Christina "called" on him. "I know! I know!" he said. "We'll help Mimi even more—we'll solve the mystery!"

"That's a great idea," said Annabelle. "But I'm not sure I'm allowed to solve real-life mysteries. And I don't think the local police will really welcome our help, do you? I mean we don't even live here."

"True," Sean agreed. "But maybe that's how we can finagle around and get some snooping done—no one will suspect us kids."

Christina had been silent all this time. Finally she spoke. "Okay, it seems impossible, it could be dangerous, and besides, we'll probably never get away from our grandparents long enough to get to work on this mystery. We have no way to get around town. We have no clues. We have no business getting involved...so, LET'S DO IT!"

Let the mystery solving begin!

She said this so loudly that it caused several people nearby to turn around and look at her. But she didn't care: Four kids; 900 stolen silver dollars; suspicious characters galore; the chance to help Mimi with her work—well, this was something she could sink her mystery-loving teeth into!

"Let the mystery solving begin!" cheered Sean. He slapped his hand on the table palm down.

"I'm in!" said Christina, plopping her hand on top of his.

"Me, too!" squealed Annabelle. She added her hand to the pile.

Grant just shook his head in disgust. "I was the first one in," he reminded them. He put his little hand on the top of the pile and mashed hard.

Just then, they all got a shock when the very same security guards that Christina and Grant had seen the previous evening paraded into the restaurant. Each had a large, heavy-looking backpack hanging from their shoulders. They marched right past the kids, plopped their backpacks in chairs, and headed for the buffet line.

"Whoooaaaaa," whispered Sean. "Good luck and great timing. It won't take us long to solve this mystery!"

Then they heard boots *clip clip clip* across the marble floor and turned to see Papa heading their way. "Oh, no," said Christina.

"Okay, kids," Papa said. "Finish up. Mimi says it's time to go to work!"

"Now?" pleaded Christina.

"Now?" begged Grant.

Papa looked down at them. He shoved his Stetson back on his head. In his booming, bass voice he announced: "NOW!"

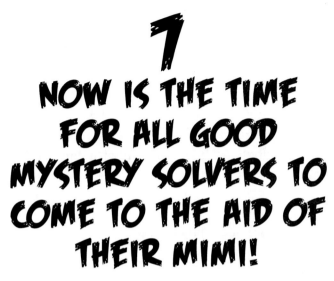

7
NOW IS THE TIME FOR ALL GOOD MYSTERY SOLVERS TO COME TO THE AID OF THEIR MIMI!

Christina and Grant knew that tone well: It meant no ifs, ands, or buts!

"I've paid your check," Papa said, agreeably. "So say goodbye to your friends and meet me and Mimi in the lobby." He spun on his boot heels to walk off.

"Papa!" Christina said suddenly, and her grandfather turned around. "Can Annabelle and Sean come with us? Their parents are tied up on business all day. We're just going to the Hershey Museum, aren't we? They would enjoy it, too." She gave Papa her sweetest grin. She knew it was always good to get both her grandparents' permission whenever possible.

Papa, of course, knew well when his granddaughter was giving him a big "sales pitch." Still, he seldom resisted. He was a tough, old hombre, but he still was a sucker when it came to his grandchildren's wishes. A smile could melt his heart as if it were made of pure chocolate.

"*Suuurrrre*," he said. He pointed to Sean and Annabelle. "Just square it with your parents first. And give them my cell phone number in case they want to find you." Papa took two business cards from his pocket and slid them across the table. They read:

PAPA
Trail Boss

Carole Marsh Mysteries
Rocking Chair Ranch
Peachtree City, Georgia
555-267-7626 (555-BOSS MAN)

"Wow, cool!" said Sean.

"Thank you so much!" said Annabelle. "We really want to help Grant and Christina..."

Papa gave her a curious look. "Help them what?" he asked suspiciously.

Christina gave her new friend a gentle kick under the table.

Annabelle blushed. "Uh, help them...help them...HAVE FUN!"

Papa just shook his head and walked off. He loved little girls, but he would never understand them.

As soon as he left, Christina began to grab her things. "Come on," she urged. "Let's go!"

Sean frowned. "But what about..."

Christina interrupted him. "We gotta go. But I didn't say we were going straight to the lobby." It was all the hint the other kids needed.

One by one, they gathered their jackets and backpacks and moseyed this way and that through the restaurant. Each one managed to pass by the table where the security guards had left their backpacks.

Annabelle tried to read a nametag on one of the backpacks, but it was too faded out.

Sean nonchalantly ran his hand over one of the backpacks and found that it was very lumpy!

Christina tripped on the carpet, causing one of the backpacks to clatter to the floor with a thud. She gasped and grabbed it up quickly and replaced it on the chair. She looked toward the buffet table and scurried away.

Lastly, Grant did the karate moves he'd learned in his classes—he was an orange belt—

across the floor, slowly working his way toward the security guards' table. For his last move, he cleverly landed under the table, where he had spotted an object. Deftly, he cupped his hand over it and rolled out from under the table. Then, he stood up and "karated" his way back across the room to the others, who had watched his antics from the doorway.

Grant joined the children just in the nick of time, because the guards were heading back to their table. When they got there, they froze, looking at their rearranged backpacks. They looked all around, then set their trays down.

"Grant!" cried Christina, when her brother met them at the door. "What did you find?"

"One guess!" Grant said proudly. The kids gathered around as he held out his hand, displaying the flat, circular object that looked like a piece of candy wrapped in silver foil. But a piece of the foil was torn, exposing the silver dollar inside.

Just as Christina reached out to take the coin to examine it, another hand appeared.

"I'll take that!" a voice said. The coin was snatched from Grant's hand. Before the kids could protest, they looked up to see that it was Emmalou Liberty. She looked very angry. "This is a warning: mind your business and don't take things that don't belong to you!" Her voice was mean and scary.

Grant didn't care; he was always fearless. "Well, maybe it doesn't belong to you either?" he challenged.

Just then Mimi walked up. She gave Emmalou Liberty a stern look. "Is there a problem here?" she demanded. She did not like the way the woman was glaring at the children. "We have returned our toboggans to the front desk."

Emmalou Liberty folded her fingers over the coin and slid it into her trench coat pocket. "No problem," she said in a fake sweet voice. "No problem at all. Have a good day." She turned and strode off.

Mimi looked at the children. She knew that something was up—something was always up with Christina and Grant! But she couldn't figure it out and she did not have time to give them the third degree. "Come on, all of you," she ordered. "I have an appointment in ten minutes. We must go."

"To the Hershey Museum?" asked Christina, hurrying to keep up with her grandmother. She wondered why they would have to be on time to a museum that was surely open all day.

"I've had a change of plans," Mimi said over her shoulder. "My first appointment is now at the Hershey Community Archives."

"What's an R Kive?" Grant asked breathlessly. When Mimi was on the move, she was hard to keep up with. Her red high heels *clack clack clacked* across the marble floor.

"It's a library," said Sean.

"Oh, no!" said Grant. "Just like school?"

Annabelle giggled.

As the four kids stood at the lobby door waiting for Papa to bring the car, and Mimi went to the concierge desk to get a map, the kids spotted the security guards leaving the dining room. They walked right over to Emmalou Liberty who began to talk rapidly and wave her arms. She pointed a finger directly at the kids. The guards turned and glared at them.

"Uh, oh," said Sean. "One thing about this mystery's solved so far."

"What?" asked Christina.

Sean sighed and said, "We've been BUSTED!"

8
BUSTED!

Papa didn't show up with their rental car—he showed up in a trolley. "All aboard!" he hollered and grinned.

"What's this?" demanded Mimi, but she was smiling.

The kids loved the bright green trolley. It reminded Christina of the streetcars they'd ridden in San Francisco. They were welcomed aboard by a singing conductor.

"Where are you headed?" the conductor asked them. They seemed to be his only customers this cold, February morning.

"Could you drop us off at the Hershey Community Archives, please?" asked Mimi, taking a seat.

"Could you drop us kids off someplace fun, PLEASE?" asked Grant. Mimi frowned.

"Why, everything at Hershey is fun, young man!" said the conductor. "The town built on chocolate is all about fun."

Grant looked out the window at the white ground. His sister knew he was wondering if the conductor meant that Hershey was literally built on top of chocolate. "That's just an expression," Christina said. "He means the town was built on the chocolate industry—right?" She looked at the smiling conductor.

"Exactly!" he said, taking his seat. He pulled a cord to ring the trolley's bell, and off they went.

As they headed down Cocoa Street (all the streets had chocolate-related names to go along with the Hershey Kisses streetlights), Papa asked, "Hey, I saw a headline in the local paper today. What's this about a local man having his coin collection stolen?"

The kids, who had been chattering away, hushed instantly in order to hear the conductor's reply.

He shook his head somberly. "Don't just know, sir," he said. "Really a bad deal. The man who owned all those coins grew up in the fine orphanage here that Mr. Milton Hershey started back in 1909. He'd purchased silver dollars from money he earned working at the Hershey

Chocolate Factory. He said when he got 1,000 of them he was going to start a scholarship in honor of Mr. Hershey. Too bad."

"Uh, excuse me," said Christina. "Do the police have any clues yet? Any idea who might have stolen the coins?"

Once more, the conductor shook his head. "Not that I've heard," he said, "and rumors fly pretty fast around a town as small as Hershey. I don't see how the culprit will get away with it."

"Why is that?" asked Mimi, always interested in a whodunit mystery.

Papa laughed. "Well, unless they vamoose, can you imagine going into a local bank with 900 silver dollars and asking to make a deposit, or exchange them for paper money? If I were the teller, I'd be a mite suspicious!"

"I'd be 100% suspicious!" said Sean. "I'd be telling on the thief so fast it would make his head spin."

"Me, too," said Annabelle. "I just can't understand why someone would be so mean. That scholarship money could help some kids go to college. I'll bet the bad guys will be in real trouble when they get caught."

"Ohhhhh, yes," the conductor assured her. "I'm sure that they will not pass Go, but Go

Directly to Jail...and it will serve them right. I guess we all agree on that?"

Just as everyone began to nod their heads, the trolley hit a bump in the street. Grant jumped in surprise and when he did, an object flew out of his jacket pocket. It rolled down the narrow aisle of the trolley, finally coming to a stop at the tip of the conductor's shoes.

The conductor bent over and retrieved the object. He held it up to his face and examined it. It appeared to be candy. But he could see a little tear in the foil wrapper, which he pulled on. In just a moment he had exposed a shiny, new silver dollar! He held it up for all to see.

"What is the meaning of this, young man?" the conductor asked sternly.

All eyes on the trolley were on Grant!— especially Mimi's and Papa's!

Grant ducked his eyes and wriggled nervously. He sat back down. Finally he looked at his sister. "I, uh, I guess I forgot to say that I picked up two objects when I was under the table in the restaurant."

"Two?" asked Mimi.

"Under what table?" said Papa. "Young man, you've got some explaining to do—and you'd better do it quick!"

9
SOME EXPLAINING TO DO!

By the time the trolley stopped at the Hershey Community Archives, Grant had "spilled his guts," as Christina would later say. He explained to his grandparents how he had been doing some karate in the restaurant dining room and accidentally rolled under the table and found a couple of pieces of what had looked like candy to him.

Christina knew they should probably "fess up" to the entire story, starting with the night before, and that Grant should not have left out the part about Emmalou Liberty. But when Papa had heard enough, he shushed them so he could think. Finally he said to Mimi, as they were hopping off the trolley: "You and the kids go on to the archives. I think I'll take this coin and head for the police station. Maybe they can pull a print, or something. It could just be an innocent, ordinary silver dollar, of course, but I'm sure they'd like to know about it."

After Papa left, the conductor said, "Ms. Marsh, I know you have some research to do. What if I personally drop off the kids at Hershey's Chocolate World. It's very educational; I know they'd have a lot of fun."

The kids began to cheer. "Please, Mimi, please?" begged Christina. "We'll behave, promise. It is educational, you know."

Their grandmother was big on anything educational, and she did have a lot of work to do. "Well, okay," she said. "But you four stay together. I will be along in about two hours. I'll call Papa on his cell phone and tell him that we'll all meet up later."

As the kids cheered again, Mimi raised her hand. "But do not get in trouble!" she made them promise. Then she gave Grant a special look. "And do not find any more stolen money, please." Grant nodded seriously and Mimi hopped off the trolley. She waved as the conductor got the trolley underway again. Christina could see that Mimi had a worried look on her face.

As the trolley sped up, Christina waved back at her grandmother and gave her a sincere,

"We'll be good" smile. Then she turned and told the other kids, "I think maybe we can learn a lot at Chocolate World, maybe enough to figure out why someone at Hershey would be stealing money that was going to such a good cause."

The other kids nodded in agreement. Before long, the conductor announced in his sing-songy voice: "HERSHEY'S CHOOOOOCOLATE WOOOOORLD!"

The kids politely thanked him for the ride, and hopped off the trolley so quickly that they did not see what was going on behind them. Boarding the trolley were the two security guards and Emmalou Liberty—and they did not look happy!

10

A WORLD OF CHOCOLATE

The kids were excited when they saw the Hershey's Chocolate World building. It was a handsome brick structure with a clock tower and candy bars with smiling faces greeted them at the entrance.

There was only one problem—each of the four kids wanted to do something different!

"Hey, look!" said Sean. "They have a Really Big 3-D Show—let's see that first!" He was a big fan of anything animated, especially if it featured characters virtually jumping right out of the screen at you.

"I'd rather take this Factory Works Experience," said Grant. "It's interactive. We can see how Hershey Kisses are made and even package our own Kisses just like they do on a production line."

Annabelle frowned. "But look at this!" She pointed to a sign about a Hersheyizer. "We can create our own personalized candy. Wouldn't that be fun?"

Christina laughed. "Well, I'd rather check out this Hershey's Bake Shop. Look at all those great desserts—YUM!"

It seemed they were at an impasse. "Well, we could flip a coin," Grant suggested, reaching in his pocket.

"Grant!" his sister squealed. "Please tell us you don't have another silver dollar!"

Her brother huffed. "Nooooo," he said. "Give me a break, will ya?"

"I have an idea," said Sean. "Let's do everything! First we'll take the tour, then we'll shop, then we'll be tired, so we'll see the movie, then we'll have a snack in the café—what do you guys think?"

"Sounds sweet to me!" said Annabelle.

"Me, too," said Christina. "We're wasting time. Papa or Mimi or both will show up before we know it. And, don't forget we still have a mystery to solve!"

Sean nodded and led the way to the entrance of the Chocolate Tour. "And I'll bet we learn something educational here that will help us do just that," he said.

"We'll see," said Christina, dubiously. She was not certain what they could learn about candy that would help them catch a thief, but it was always possible. For herself, she was doing what she usually did—keeping an eye out for what Mimi called "persons of interest." She knew that meant people who might look or act suspicious. But her grandmother always reminded her that you couldn't "judge a book by its cover" and that her granddaughter should keep an open mind as well as open eyes.

Pretty soon, Christina realized that she had been daydreaming and the other kids had left her behind. She raced to catch up—chocolate was her favorite thing! That's why she never saw the two security guards and Emmalou Liberty enter the building.

The two guards and Miss Liberty exchanged hand signals, and each went in a different direction: one to tail those four "highly suspicious" kids; another to speak to the manager; and the last to buy snacks in the café—even adults get hungry for chocolate!

11

WHO KNEW CHOCOLATE WAS HISTORIC?

After the kids saw the Really Big 3D Movie, they decided they needed a snack and went to the Kit Kat Gimme a Break Café to have a snack.

"So did you learn anything about chocolate that would help us solve the Silver Dollar Mystery?" Christina teased Sean. The kids had begun to refer to the mysterious mystery by that name.

Sean stuffed another scoop of ice cream sundae with chocolate syrup into his mouth. "Well, I didn't know chocolate had such a history," he admitted. "I think my teacher would be interested in all that historic stuff about chocolate in Spain and in the New World."

Grant munched on a chocolate cupcake with chocolate frosting. "Maybe you can take a Hershey Bar to school for Show and Tell?"

"Well, I was surprised to learn that chocolate comes from the cacao bean," said Annabelle.

"I just can't figure out how anything we learned helps us," admitted Christina. "Mr. Milton Hershey was sure an interesting and smart man. I wish he were still alive to help us. I don't think he'd like such a theft in the town that he built."

Grant wiped a dribble of chocolate from his chin and snapped his fingers. "I have an idea! Let's be philosophers like Mr. Hershey!"

Annabelle giggled. "I think you mean **philanthropist**, Grant?"

Grant just shrugged his shoulders. "Well, one of those funny words that begin with an 'f'."

"Philanthropist starts with a PH," Christina told her brother. "It's a person who gives time or money to help others. It was cool how he took care of the town during the Great Depression and started that orphanage for boys." She looked at her brother curiously. "What do you have in mind?"

Grant motioned the other kids closer and whispered. "What if we take the money we were going to spend shopping today and instead give it to the poor man who had his silver dollars stolen? We could meet him and ask him some questions." Annabelle leaned back and sighed. "I don't know," she said. "I was looking forward to buying my mom some candy. But I guess I can do that another day."

"Sure," said Sean, "why not? I'm in."

"Me too," agreed Christina.

The kids piled their hard-earned money into the center of the table. After they paid their bill, they would have just about twenty dollars left.

"Well, that's a start," said Christina.

"Hey, how about we go by the bank and get these bills exchanged for silver dollars?" suggested Sean. "I'll bet that would make that man happy."

"Great idea!" said Christina, cleaning up their mess. "Let's hurry. I saw a bank nearby, but how are we going to find out where the man who had his money stolen lives?"

"Don't you remember?" said Sean. "It was in the newspaper—he lived on Chocolate Avenue...or was it Cocoa Way...or maybe it was

Hershey Street?" He threw up his hands in exasperation.

The other kids giggled. "Oh, great!" said Annabelle. "Half the streets in Hershey have candy names, so that's no help at all."

Christina stood up and led the way to the entrance. The kids were dashing out to find a bank so fast that they didn't notice that they were still being followed—this time by someone dressed as a candy bar...walking a dog.

Actually, Christina did turn around and notice the dog because it started barking at them. "Hey, what a cute dog," said Annabelle. "It's a lab, but what kind?"

Grant didn't even turn around. He just called back over his shoulder, "A chocolate lab, silly!"

Whatever kind of lab it was, the kids didn't realize that it was "sniffing them out!"

THE SWEET SMELL OF CHOCOLATE

The kids loved the sights and the sounds of downtown Hershey. They especially liked the streetlamps shaped just like Hershey's Kisses, even including the "plume" of paper streamer that let you know it was a real Hershey's Kiss!

"How do you get rich enough to build a whole town?" Sean asked Christina as they slowly walked along the snowy streets.

"Failure's a good place to start," Christina surprised him by saying.

"Huh?"

As they walked along—noses in the air, sniffing happily—Christina explained, "Mr. Hershey was like a lot of successful people, Mimi told me. He had plenty of hard times and hard knocks—before, during, and even after he found success."

The kids plopped down on a bench and continued to savor the chocolatey smell wafting down on them along with a light sprinkle of snow. "Tell us more," said Annabelle, who loved to read biographies of famous people.

Christina enjoyed playing teacher. "Well," she began. "For one thing, he was born in Pennsylvania just before the Civil War. It was a scary time, even for people who lived in the country like the Hershey family. His family was Mennonite, so as a boy, Milton and his little sister Serena had a very strict childhood and worked hard on the family farm. They moved around a lot and so Milton had to change schools all the time; he wasn't a very good student. Then, one day, his little sister died."

"Boy, all that sounds pretty bad," said Sean.

Christina shook her head. "Trust me—the worst was yet to come. Milton finally got a job as an apprentice to a candymaker. That's how he learned the confectioner trade. Then he tried striking out on his own, but he had failure after failure, until he finally succeeded in making caramels."

"I love caramels!" said Grant, rubbing his tummy.

"Not me," said Christina. "They stick in my braces. But Mr. Hershey was so successful that he sold his caramel company for $1 million! That was really a lot of money back then!"

"So he got out of the candy business after that?" asked Annabelle.

"No!" said Christina. "He used that money to build a new chocolate factory! And he had this great idea to add milk to the chocolate. The candy he made was delicious. Everyone loved it and couldn't get enough."

"Just like us!" said Grant, sniffing the air again.

"Yeah, isn't it time for lunch?" asked Sean.

"We're supposed to be on our way to the bank and do a good deed," Christina reminded him, standing up.

"Maybe we could go back to Hershey's Chocolate World first?" hinted Annabelle. "Then go to the bank?"

Christina hesitated. "Papa did give me $20 for lunch. So, sure, but let's still go to the bank first. It's just across the street."

"Okay!" said Sean, leading the way across the crosswalk. "Bank...Chocolate World...then find the man whose money was stolen and give him some back—right?"

Christina sighed. She was certain that she would never win this battle. "Suuuuuuuure," she said, sounding just like her Uncle Michael who said that when someone asked him to do something he didn't really want to do, but he was a good sport and did it anyway.

As they marched single-file into the bank, Christina was last. She had a funny feeling—intuition, her grandmother would call it. She felt like someone was following them. Just before she went into the bank, she turned around and looked.

Chocolate Avenue was quiet this cold, winter's day. The only thing she really saw were three people, snuggled down in their coats and hats, sitting on the bench the kids had just vacated. Their heads were bent down like they were napping.

Christina looked up and down the street, then shrugged her shoulders. She turned to catch up with the other kids. That's why she never saw the three bench-sitters lift their heads as soon as Christina had gone inside. Quickly, they jumped from the bench and padded across the snow-covered street and up the steps of the bank where they secretively peered inside to see what "those darn kids" (as they called them) were up to!

Kisses light the night!

13

A LITTLE BANKING BUSINESS

The kids headed immediately to the counter where a teller looked down at them and smiled. "How can I help you kids today?" she asked. "And why aren't you in school, come to think of it?"

"We're strangers in these parts, ma'am," drawled Grant, sounding just like his grandfather. "Just passing through. Gonna eat a little chocolate and mosey along on our way."

The teller laughed. "But do you have banking business?"

Christina decided she'd better butt in. "Yes, maam," she said. "We have some cash dollars that we want to exchange for silver dollars."

At this, the teller not only looked a little suspicious, but also quietly pushed a red button beneath the counter. This alerted the manager. Mr. Jasper made a quick appearance at her side.

"And what can we do for you children today?" he asked. He gripped folded hands in front of him and bent slightly from his waist. It was a look that Christina disliked —as if kids were a pain in the neck and not to be taken seriously. But as Papa would say, "Money talks." So Christina quickly spread her ten dollar bills across the counter.

"I'd like to exchange these for silver dollars," she said firmly.

Mr. Jasper frowned, then nodded at the teller, who quickly scooped up the dollars and shoved a shiny stack of silver dollars over to Christina. She scooped them up and stuffed them in her jacket pocket.

Without a word, each of the other kids quickly lined up behind Christina and did the same. "Thank you," each one said, and then turned and headed for the door.

Just as they were about to leave, Christina overheard Mr. Jasper say to the teller. "Seems like there's quite a run on silver dollars in Hershey these days, hey?"

Christina spun around. "Excuse me," she said. "What do you mean?"

Mr. Jasper just smiled. "Oh, nothing that would interest you kids."

The curly-headed teller looked like she was dying to say something!

Christina thought fast. "It is okay if we get some water?" she asked, pointing to a silver water fountain in the corner.

The bank manager frowned, but nodded, then hurried away. Christina headed for the water fountain, and the other kids, looking puzzled, followed her. As soon as Mr. Jasper vanished to his office, Christina made a beeline to the teller counter.

"We know about the theft," she told the teller. "That's why we came to get these silver dollars; we want to give them to the poor man who had his money stolen. Is there something we should know before we do that?"

The teller's curls bounced as she glanced back to make sure Mr. Jasper was still in his office. "Oh, kids, it's all the talk!" she said, leaning over the counter to whisper to them. "Mr. Daniels— the man who had his money stolen—is so sweet. He grew up in the school Mr. Hershey and his wife started long ago. Later, he worked in the chocolate factory and retired. He never married or had children. But he did bank here and each week he would cash his paycheck and get part of it in silver dollars and take them home. We always wondered what he did with them."

"Seems like he shoulda left them in the bank," said Grant. "Maybe they wouldn't have been stolen then."

"I know, I know!" said the teller. "Mr. Jasper asked him about that one day, but Mr. Daniels didn't want to discuss it. The weird thing," she said, leaning so far over the counter, the kids thought she might fall head first on them, "is that we kept tabs on how many silver dollars he got all those years—and it was a lot!"

Christina gave the woman a curious look. "Well, the paper said 900 silver dollars were stolen—that is a lot."

The teller shook her curls once more. "But there were a lot more than that!"

The kids couldn't stand it!

"How many?" asked Sean.

"Maybe 9,000?" guessed Annabelle.

"More than that?" asked Grant.

Before the teller could answer,

Mr. Jasper's office door opened. The teller sat back up in her swivel chair, and the kids hurried to the door.

"Thanks, again," Christina called back to the teller, who gave her a wink.

"Any time," the teller said, then repeated as if giving a big hint: "ANY time!"

When the kids left the bank, they looked down at all the big footprints on the snow-covered steps.

"I think we were followed!" said Grant.

"Why?" asked Sean, puzzled.

"No one came in the bank after us," said Grant. "And our feet aren't that big."

"I knew my instincts were right!" said Christina.

"What do you mean?" asked Annabelle.

"I had a feeling we were being followed when we came in the bank," Christina explained. She looked up and down the street, but saw no one. It was pretty cold to be out unless you had to be.

Sean patted his jacket pocket. "Maybe someone wants to steal our silver dollars," he said.

"I'm freezing!" said Annabelle. "Let's go back to Chocolate World and get warm—please?!"

Christina nodded. "Just watch your pockets!" she warned, as the kids dashed down the steps of the bank. Just then, a trolley came by and they waved it down.

"You kids better get in here!" said the conductor. "It's getting colder by the minute. Where do you want to go?"

"CHOCOLATE WORLD!" squealed Grant, scampering aboard. As the other kids followed him, the conductor laughed.

"You kids jingle like silver bells!" he said. "What's that all about?"

The kids looked at one another, then stared at Grant, who this time, knew not to confess that they were loaded with silver dollars!

14

CHOCOLATE WORLD REDUX

On the trolley, Christina made a quick call to Mimi to tell her what they were doing. Her grandmother told her she was tied up at the archives, which Christina knew meant that Mimi was having fun doing research, and that Papa had gone back to the hotel for a nap.

"Just stay in and stay warm and stay out of trouble!" Mimi warned her granddaughter. "Let me know what you're up to later and we'll meet for Chocolate Tea at the Hotel Hershey!"

When the trolley arrived at Hershey's Chocolate World, everyone bounded off and dashed inside. The kids went through the gift shop to get to the café.

"Wow!" said Grant, as soon as they entered the doorway. "This is like dying and going to

Chocolate Heaven!" They were surrounded by chocolate! It seemed like every kind of chocolate or type of candy that the Hershey Company made was for sale.

"Look at that!" squealed Annabelle. She pointed to the Hershey Bakery with its display coolers filled with colorfully-decorated cookies and cupcakes.

"Food first!" said Christina, sounding a little like her mom, who always wanted them to eat nutritiously.

"Up here!" shouted Sean, leading them up a flight of stairs to the café.

After they all ordered steaming bowls of chicken noodle soup, ham and cheese sandwiches, and enormous mugs of hot cocoa topped with great dollops of whipped cream, they settled on a table overlooking the chocolate world beneath them.

"So finish the story of Mr. Hershey, Christina," Annabelle asked her friend.

Christina squinted her eyes, trying to remember where she left off. "Oh, yeah!" she said, snapping her fingers. "Mr. Hershey was quite a chocolate **entrepreneur**. He was brave and pressed on, improving the factory and tackling problems and opportunities as quickly as you might hit tennis balls back over a net. He was happy and now he was a success instead of a failure. He even got married."

"Wow!" said Annabelle. "Lucky lady to marry the King of Chocolate!"

Christina smiled. "Mr. Hershey would say that he was the lucky one. They built a big home and traveled all over the world. But his wife, Kitty, got sick and she never got well. She died and Mr. Hershey was very sad. He finally gave all his money to the Milton Hershey School he and Kitty had built."

"And he kept making chocolate?" asked Sean, who had a whipped cream mustache.

"Oh, yeah!" said Christina. "He invented new kinds of candy like Hershey's Kisses!"

"One of my favorites!" said Annabelle.

"They're ALL my favorites!" said Grant. He had gobbled down his lunch so he could head downstairs and start shopping—usually not his favorite thing, but he was making an exception today!

When they finished their lunch, they went downstairs and tried out the Hersheyizer, a funny-looking candy contraption. First they put on hard hats and selected the candy they wanted. Then the clerk dumped the candy in the Hersheyizer and it traveled through tubes and funnels until it came out into a special box.

"Boy, now we have treats whenever we need them," said Sean.

The kids paid for the candy and headed to the Factory Works. There they watched chocolate treats go through an elaborate assembly line, up and down conveyors until they came out in a brightly-colored box shaped like a gear.

"There's just candy everywhere!" said Grant.

"You can never have too much chocolate," said Christina.

"Who said that?" asked Sean. "Mr. Hershey?"

Christina laughed. "Maybe," she said. "But I really meant Mimi—she loves chocolate!"

Next, they headed for the Hershey's Factory Tour.

Grant looked all around. "We really get to go into the factory?"

Christina steered Grant toward the entranceway to the Chocolate Tour. They all headed up a carpeted ramp. Along the way were big displays and even television monitors telling how cacao is grown and harvested.

"Aw, this seems boring," said Grant. "More school stuff. Is there a test at the end?"

"No," said Annabelle, with a little giggle. "There's a ride!"

And soon, they came to a turntable type floor. One by one, an attendant directed the kids to walk across the moving floor and climb into "the first car" that was heading their way. Staggering left and right and giggling, the kids finally made their way to the chocolate-colored open cars and climbed aboard—Grant and Annabelle in front; Christina and Sean in back...and the train lurched ahead.

They were so excited that they did not see the three adults squeeze into the car behind them.

Factory Fun!

90

15

A KISS IS JUST A KISS

At first the cars, on a jerky track, pulled them past some singing cows.

"This seems like something for little kids," Christina complained to Sean.

But soon, the tour went right past big displays that looked just like a real chocolate factory and explained how chocolate was made. It started out with cocoa beans and went through all the sorting and grinding and roasting and cooking stages required to even begin to start making something that tasted sweet and good.

"This tour's quite an **excursion**. I never knew making candy was so complicated," Sean said. When the car lurched again, he slung his arm over the back of the car to hold on.

"Me either," said Christina. "No wonder the real Hershey's Factory is so enormous."

The next part of the process, when the milk was added, looked yummiest. Giant machines stirred the chocolate which was then poured into molds to make bars or squirted onto conveyor belts in little "kisses." Even the packaging machines were marvels, doing their job so fast you could hardly see how it actually happened.

Christina was so fascinated that she decided to make a Chocolate-Making Scrapbook and take it to school for a report.

When the chocolate scent grew even stronger, and displays of other candy appeared, Grant and Annabelle threw their arms up in the air as if they were on a rollercoaster and cheered!

Just as their car jolted out of the darkness, they hit a bump and Sean's lips brushed Christina's cheek.

What did Christina do? She screamed!

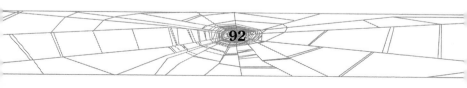

16

HELP!

"Sorry!" said Sean, shocked. "I didn't mean..."

Christina spun around, "It's not that," she said. "Someone just put their hand in my jacket pocket! I think they were trying to steal my silver dollars!"

Sean spun around too. The adults who had been in the car behind them were long gone. "But how could someone know you had silver dollars in your pocket?"

"What's wrong?" asked Annabelle, hopping out of her car. She staggered on the moving carpet to the stairs, where an attendant handed her some Hershey's Kisses.

"Waaaiiit for meeeeeeeee!" squealed Grant. He pretended that the carpet was going to carry him away, but an attendant helped him to the steps and handed him Hershey's Kisses of his own.

Sean and Christina followed, waving away the offer of candy as they trudged up the steps to the ramp above. Quickly, Christina took the silver dollars out of her pocket and counted them.

"They're all there," she said in relief. "But that was pretty rude and audacious, for someone to try to steal money right out of my pocket!"

"I agree," said Sean. "Something's just not right about all this, you know?"

And soon, they all knew. Why? Because at the bottom of the ramp exiting the Chocolate Tour stood a policeman.

"I'd like to have a word with you," he said to the children. "Right over here. Right now."

Shocked and scared, the kids dutifully followed the officer. If someone had been following them...and trying to steal from them, then why were THEY the ones in trouble?

WE GOT TROUBLE, RIGHT HERE IN CHOCOLATE CITY!

"What's wrong, officer?" Christina asked, as soon as the policeman led them to a small table near the offices. They all sat down.

"That's what I'd like for you to tell me," said the officer. He seemed stern but kind. But Christina worried that Mimi and Papa would be stern and not kind if they found out that the kids had been arrested for something. That probably did not qualify as "stay out of trouble," in her grandmother's mind...not at all!

"We don't understand," Sean said. "We just took the tour; that's all. We didn't cause any problems, sir."

Grant looked sad. "I'm sorry if we screamed too loud," he said. "We were just excited and having fun." He looked over at Annabelle, who nodded, her big blue eyes near tears.

The policeman laughed. "It's okay," he said. "That's no problem. We want you to have fun at Chocolate World–that's what it's here for. But one of the attendants overheard one of you say that someone was trying to steal your money. Now we can't have that, can we?"

The kids all shook their heads.

Then the officer grew more serious. "And it was noticed that you paid for your lunch, and your candy purchases, and your theater tickets...with silver dollars." He looked from child to child. "And with what's been going on in Hershey, well, you might say that did attract a little attention."

Christina knew he meant *suspicion*. "We know about the theft," she explained. "But we have a reason to have these silver dollars. We did get them at the bank with our own money."

Now the officer shook his head up and down. "Oh, I know, I know," he said. "I already checked. I'm not accusing you of anything. I just wanted to make sure everything was all right. We couldn't help but notice that you kids were alone. I mean, no adult is with you, right?"

"Uh," Christina began, knowing that how she explained this would be important. "We are alone—right now. But my grandmother and grandfather are here in Hershey. They're just busy right now. But they plan to meet us later."

"When?" asked the officer. He looked doubtful.

"Right after we visit the Hershey Museum," volunteered Sean. "Maybe you can tell us where it is?"

The policeman relaxed. "It's just across the street. I can walk you over there."

"Oh, that's okay, really," said Christina. "We can get there. I want to work on a Chocolate-Making Scrapbook for a school project. And I just need a little more information."

The officer looked relieved. "Well, that sounds harmless enough. There are people on duty at the museum who can answer your questions. What if I just walk you to the door?"

The kids nodded and followed the policeman to the exit. They couldn't help but notice that all the other visitors had stopped to stare at them and whisper. Christina was so embarrassed. She figured everyone thought they were being kicked out of Chocolate World. Oh, well, she thought, she couldn't do anything about other people drawing the wrong conclusions.

At the door, the officer dug in his shirt pocket and handed Christina his card. It said:

Christina giggled. "Really, that's your name?"

The officer smiled and shrugged. "So this is the perfect place for me, right?"

"It sure is," said Grant, peering over his sister's shoulder at the card. "Officer Chocolate—that's really funny," he added and giggled.

"Thanks, Officer Chocolate!" said Annabelle. She giggled, too, and went out the door, snugging her scarf up around her neck. It was really cold.

"Appreciate it, Officer Chocolate," said Sean. He did not giggle, but he did smile.

Officer Chocolate blushed. "Okay, you kids, get on to the museum. I'm going to watch you until I actually see you go in the door."

Christina nodded. "Thanks," she said. And then she turned and followed the other kids. When she looked back, sure enough, she could see the policeman straining to see them through the foggy window.

"Brrrrrrrrrrr," she mumbled under her breath and dashed into the Hershey Museum. She did not look back again or she would have seen Officer Chocolate meet up with the two security guards and Emmalou Liberty, who looked like they were plotting something and were up to no good!

18
LONGITUDE OR LATITUDE?

"Did we really want to come to the museum?" Sean asked, as soon as they were all inside.

"Not me," said Grant. "It's kind of dark in here."

"Grant!" said Annabelle. "You haven't even looked around. I'm sure there's plenty of interesting stuff in a museum devoted to chocolate."

"YOU'RE RIGHT!" boomed a voice behind them. "There's lots to see in here! Mr. Hershey liked things that people used long ago. He even bought two collections of artifacts—one was Native American artifacts and the other a group of things used by early settlers in Pennsylvania. And then there's a lot about the chocolate factory and the people who worked there in the past."

The man moved behind the counter and took their money for their tickets. He only looked a little surprised when he saw that they were paying with silver dollars.

"Thataway," he said. "Let me know if you have any questions."

"What was this place before it was a museum?" asked Grant, heading off. "It doesn't look like a museum to me."

The man laughed. "It used to be a skating rink!"

"That's cool!" said Annabelle, following Grant. "I want to come back to Hershey when it's summer and go to the amusement park and the zoo."

"That sounds like fun," Grant replied.

"Well, let's take a quick look at the museum and then we can go find some more hot chocolate," Sean suggested. "I imagine our parents will be looking for us pretty soon," he said to Annabelle.

When Christina was quiet, the kids all turned and looked at her. "You know," she said. "We've been spending our silver dollars. I'm down to three."

"Us, too," said Sean. "But once we traded our paper dollars in, how were we going to pay our way to eat lunch and get in the attractions if we didn't?"

"True," said Christina. "I wish we'd gotten half in silver dollars and saved them, then we could have used our paper dollars to pay for stuff."

"It would attract less suspicion," Annabelle agreed.

"Hey, look over here!" Grant called. He was halfway across the giant hall.

The other kids ran to join him and found Grant "clocking in" using a realistic-looking factory time card.

"Hey, where did you get that?" asked Sean, eager to try it for himself.

Soon all the kids had "clocked in" and were donning factory uniforms from metal lockers. The next step in "pretending" to be a Hershey factory worker was to enter the Longitude Department.

"Wow, look at this!" said Annabelle. The display showed large, brown bathtub-shaped tubs workers had to fill with chocolate.

Grant tried to lift a bucket that simulated the weight of a bucket of chocolate. "This is some kind of heavy!" he complained. In fact, he couldn't even move it.

Sean tried and barely pulled the bucket off its perch. "Man, imagine having to lift bucketfuls of chocolate this heavy all day long," he said.

"Yeah," added Christina, tugging on

the brown tub. It would not even budge—and it was empty!

"Chocolate-making's hard word," said Annabelle. "Maybe things are more automated these days? I sure hope so."

"Read this!" said Grant. He pointed to one of the "oral history" signs around the display that quoted what real workers had said about their jobs in the Hershey factory. It said: *New workers were called greenies—and if you turned your back, someone might play a trick and hide your chocolate bucket or scoop in a tub full of chocolate!*

"Where you couldn't see it," added Annabelle. "That's mean."

"And you'd sure get messy getting it back out," said Christina. "Especially since there's no telling how many tubs you might have to check!"

"I guess it's like getting to be part of the club," suggested Sean. "Sort of an initiation."

Next they read an oral history sign that said early cocoa beans had come to the factory from Africa. *Sometimes we found guns, bullets, or even sandals in the bags of beans*, read a card.

"Listen to how hot it was!" said Annabelle. "Some days up to 130 degrees!"

"Or cold in the wrapping part of the plant," said Sean, pointing to another card.

"I guess that's the problem with

chocolate," said Christina. "First you have to get it warm enough to melt...then you have to get it cold enough so it won't!"

Next they wandered over to a display that talked more about the long, hard work it took to make chocolate, especially in the early days of the plant. Like any factory, the workers demanded better working conditions. Even though Mr. Hershey was known as a good employer, times were changing.

"Now, just look at this!" said Annabelle. "For a long time the women didn't make as much money as the men—that's not fair."

"Well," said Sean. "Men couldn't get some of the easier jobs, like wrapping. That wasn't fair, either."

"I guess that's why they joined labor **unions**," said Christina.

"What's a union?" asked Grant.

"It's an organization you join that fights for your interests at your job," his sister explained. "You also pay dues to belong to it."

"You mean they fight for things like shorter hours or better wages?" guessed Sean.

"Or safer working conditions," said Christina. "See—back then they didn't even know that the loud noises the plant machinery made could make you lose your hearing. Today, they wear earplugs."

"Hey, look at this," said Annabelle. "It said the noise was so loud that lots of workers learned to read lips so they could 'talk' while they worked."

"Well, at least Mr. Hershey made sure that the town had good houses and gardens and doctors and schools and things the families needed," said Sean, looking over the next display.

"Better than that," said Christina, "he kept everyone working during the Great Depression. While lots of folks were going hungry, the people at Hershey kept their jobs."

Christina thought it was fun to learn new things. The museum was even more interesting than she had expected. But as the other kids walked on, she spotted the man who had sold them tickets talking to someone who had come into the museum. They were both pointing toward the children, and Christina discovered she could read lips too:

Up to no good.
Loaded with silver dollars.
No adult with them.
Call the cops?

"Hey, gang," she called to the others. "I think it's time to vamoose!"

19

EXIT STAGE LEFT!

They all broke into a fast run until they found themselves trapped in a back corner of the museum. Sean spied daylight behind some crates and said, "Come on—I think a door is open!"

Sure enough, an exit door was propped open, probably because someone had been moving items in or out from the large moving truck parked nearby. Since whoever that was wasn't around, the kids raced out the door, down the steps, and back across the street to the trolley that was just about to pull off.

"Wait for us!" cried Annabelle.

The conductor turned and smiled. "Where did you kids come from?" he said, as they boarded. "It's too cold to be outside."

There was no one on the bus but them. The conductor said he was headed to the Hotel Hershey for his last pick-up of the day.

"That's great," said Christina. "That's where we're staying and we're supposed to meet my grandparents for tea, I mean chocolate." She paused. "Or chocolate tea—I forget what you call it."

The conductor laughed. "It's the Hotel Hershey's famous afternoon Chocolate Tea. You'll love it."

"Can we ask you a question?" Christina asked shyly.

The conductor looked amused. "Of course you can, young lady. I am well-versed in everything Hershey. Go ahead and ask away!"

"Well it's not exactly that kind of question," Christina said. "It's about the recent theft."

The conductor looked serious. "Yes, that's a shame. Not like Hershey at all. We just don't have much bad stuff happen in the Sweetest Place on Earth."

"Feels more like the Coldest Place on Earth," grumbled Grant. He pulled his hat down over his ears. Even in the warm car, he could see his breath make white smoke in the chilly air.

Annabelle and Sean played tic-tac-toe on the frosty windows. Grant went to snuggle up beside them.

Christina felt like this was her big chance. "Can you tell us where Mr. Daniels lives?" she asked the conductor. "We'd really like to meet him."

"Hmmm," said the conductor. "And why is that? I mean you're a bunch of kids on vacation, and Mr. Daniels is a retired factory worker, and not in good health. What do you have in mind?"

Christina hesitated. Finally, she blurted out the best explanation she could think of. "We just feel sorry for him. We actually have some gifts for him. We want to drop them off at his house. We won't stay long or bother him."

The conductor looked suspicious. "And what kinds of gifts are these?" He glanced around. "I don't see any packages."

"Uh, they're small gifts," said Christina. "We have them in our pockets."

When the conductor looked, he could indeed see a bulge in each kid's jacket pocket. It made Christina sad to think how much smaller the "bulges" were now than earlier in the day.

The conductor stroked his chin thoughtfully. "Well, Mr. Daniels does live on my route. I'm a little early. Maybe I could stop and let you run in—real quick, though, then jump back on the trolley. Promise, young lady?"

"PROMISE!" Christina said so loudly the other kids looked up. She ran back to explain what was going to happen. The kids were so excited that they moved to seats near the door and waited for the trolley to stop and the conductor to open the door and give them the word to "Go!"

When that finally happened, the cold hit them in their faces hard. Sleet stuck to their eyelashes. Quickly, they scampered up the few steps to the small porch of the small house. A lone light burned in the front window.

More bravely than she felt, Christina banged the door knocker—it was a brass Hershey's Kiss—and so cold she feared her fingers would stick to it.

As they waited, she glanced around and saw the conductor fiddling with some paperwork, but he glanced up every few seconds and she knew that they didn't have much time to say "Howdy" to Mr. Daniels and give him their small tokens of money to make him feel better, they hoped.

Suddenly, Grant got a funny look on his face and began to back away from the house.

"What is it, Grant?" Christina asked her brother. She was afraid he was going to be sick. Maybe he'd consumed too much chocolate?

Grant shook his head slowly, his hat falling down around his eyes. With one hand he lifted his hat back up and peered through the gauzy curtains once more. "I don't think we need to go in there," he told his sister. His voice quivered.

"Why not?!" said Christina. She tried to see what Grant was looking at, but a shutter blocked her view. Then suddenly the kids moved over to where Grant had been standing and looked.

"Ohmygosh!" said Annabelle.

"What the heck?!" said Sean.

"Something's wrong. Very wrong!" said Christina.

The four children turned on the slippery steps and fled back to the trolley. They raced up the steps and trounced down the aisle to the back of the bus.

"Mission accomplished?" asked the conductor.

"Uh, Mr. Daniels didn't seem to be home," said Christina. "We'll try again later. But thank you, anyway." She realized that her voice was quivering too, but not from the cold.

"No problem," said the conductor and took his seat.

At the back of the trolley, as it chugged toward the Hotel Hershey, the kids huddled and whispered.

"Mr. Daniels might or might not be home," said Grant, finally. "But his money sure is!"

"LOTS OF IT!" said Annabelle and Sean together and so loudly that the conductor turned to look at them. The kids just waved.

Christina shook her head. "I've never seen so many silver dollars in my whole life. I didn't even know that there were that many!" She paused.

"What is it?" asked Sean. He did not like the look on Christina's face.

"You don't think," she began, then hesitated. "You don't think Mr. Daniels is his own thief?"

Not another word was spoken the entire ride to the hotel. Christina and Grant had encountered plenty of mysteries before, but this was certainly one of the most curious. Maybe the most curious of all!

20

CHOCOLATE TEA

It should have been a joyous occasion. It was their last night in Hershey. Mimi had made special reservations for them to enjoy the Hotel Hershey's special afternoon Chocolate Tea.

Indeed, it should have been extra special because Mimi had phoned Annabelle's and Sean's parents to make sure they could go to the tea as well. The blowing snow outside made it the perfect winter postcard kind of day to be inside a lovely historic hotel with a blazing fire and tea and cake and cookies and chocolate of all sorts and endless mugs of cocoa awaiting.

The kids were starving; it had been hours since lunch. But none of them seemed to have much of an appetite.

"What's wrong?" asked Papa. He scoffed up another handful of Hershey's Kisses and slipped one down the back of Mimi's blouse.

"What was that?" she asked, turning and giving Papa a flirty smile. She captured the Kiss before it went further and set it by her plate. "Is something wrong?" she asked the children. "You kids are so quiet. Are you just tired? No one's coming down with a cold, are they?"

Christina answered for them all. "No," she promised. She didn't want her grandmother to worry. "I guess we've just had a busy day. Thanks for the tea, Mimi, it's really nice." She ate a bite of chocolate just to convince her grandmother everything was fine."

"Yes, thank you," said Annabelle. "It's quite delicious."

"Me, too," chimed in Sean. "I mean, thanks. I love Kisses." He popped one in his mouth while Mimi wondered why her granddaughter had just blushed.

"Well, my tummy hurts," said Grant. "I'm gonna lay on that sofa by the fire."

When he got up and walked off, the other kids followed him. "Let me know if he feels worse," Mimi called after them.

"Probably just too much chocolate," said Papa, popping another Kiss.

Mimi slapped his hand. "Kids aren't the only ones who can get tummy aches, you know."

"Yes, ma'am!" said Papa, shoving his plate away with a grin.

"Grant, are you really sick?" Christina asked, as her brother rolled on the sofa. "What are you up to?"

Quickly, Grant popped up and patted the sofa cushions for the others to join him. "No, of course not!" he said. "I just wanted to get away so we could talk. You know, Mimi will make us eat dinner and go to bed soon. We have an early flight tomorrow. Surely this can't be the first time we leave a place with a mystery unsolved. Can it, Christina?" He looked like he might cry.

Christina sighed. "I'm sorry to say maybe so, Grant," she said sadly. "I hate it. I even heard Mimi say she'd had a great trip but the town of Hershey was so sweet that she didn't have a clue what to write a mystery about. She said she might not."

"Oh, no!" said Annabelle. "I was really looking forward to reading it. Maybe even being in it," she added.

"Bummer!" said Sean. "Maybe you guys just aren't as good of mystery-solvers as you told us." He had a twinkle in his eye, but to Grant and Christina those were fighting words!

"Not true!" said Grant. He jumped up and did one of his wildest and crazy karate moves. "We can solve anything!" As he spun and jabbed, a silver dollar whipped out of his pocket and rolled across the marble floor. Everyone seemed to stop and look at the appearance of the strange object at the Chocolate Tea.

"Yeah, we can solve anything except what to tell Mimi and Papa about that coin," said Christina. "And that I have NO satisfactory solution for!"

21

THREE COINS IN THE FOUNTAIN

But that was not the explanation that the kids had to worry about. As the silver dollar rolled across the floor toward the fountain, Papa stopped it with the toe of his boot. With hands on hips, he looked down at the four children who had scrambled after it. As they fell on the floor to try to grab the coin, more silver dollars spilled from their pockets.

"What's this?!" asked Mimi. She looked totally confused as she surveyed the scene on the floor.

"That's what I'd like to know," said a new voice. Everyone turned to see Officer Charles Chocolate standing in the doorway of the Fountain Lobby!

Behind him marched the two security guards, Miss Emmalou Liberty, the curly-headed bank teller, and Mr. Jasper, the bank manager.

"We're in big trouble now," Christina said quietly to the others.

"Stand up," Papa ordered.

The kids scrambled to their feet and the adults made a circle around them. Christina felt it was going to be quite an inquisition. She had a **rancid** taste in her mouth, and felt sick to her stomach.

Officer Chocolate began: "As everyone in this room knows, Mr. Daniels was a long time Hershey employee who recently had some valuable silver dollars stolen."

"Then I think you should look at those people!" Grant surprised everyone by shouting. He pointed to the two security guards. "They have bags of silver dollars—we saw them!" The other kids nodded rapidly. Mimi and Papa looked more confused than ever.

The two men came forward. They did not look worried at all. In fact, they looked amused.

"Of course we do," said one of the men. "We're the ones who pick up and deliver money from the banks around here."

"But to take to breakfast?" asked Sean. "We know you brought bags of silver dollars in here because that's where we got our first ones."

Now everyone looked puzzled, except the kids.

"Your first silver dollars?" asked Officer Chocolate. He wore a suspicious expression on his face.

"Yes," said Annabelle bravely. "Grant and Christina saw those men counting and wrapping money in one of the rooms in this very hotel. The next morning, when we tried to investigate, we—well, Grant, actually—found a couple of coins that fell out of their bags. Doesn't that seem a little guilty to anyone besides us kids?"

All eyes focused on the security guards. "Well, it would, I agree," said one of the men, looking a little nervous. "Except that we were given those two bags of silver dollars to guard here at the hotel."

"And to wrap," said the other guard. "So they would not look like silver dollars, except to nosy kids like you."

Now, Papa stepped forward. "Whoa, there, little buddy!" he said to the guard, who was not little at all, and certainly no friend of Papa's now that he had called his grandkids and their friends "nosy." "I think an explanation is in order," Papa said.

Everyone stared at Officer Chocolate, but he looked lost. "Uh," he began.

Surprisingly, Mr. Jasper, the bank manager, now stepped forward. "What those two men say is true," he said. "Mr. Daniels was a long time customer of our bank. We wanted to help figure out who stole his money. I personally asked these men to hold some silver dollars for me. We hoped to make them 'available,' so to speak, hoping the crook would strike again, only this time we'd catch him."

For a moment, the room was silent. Then Sean spoke up. "Well, maybe the thief is not a man at all. How about her?!" He turned and pointed at Emmalou Liberty, who had been standing quietly on the sidelines.

Officer Chocolate turned to the woman. "Ma'am?" he asked. "Do you have anything to do with this, uh, this mess?"

Miss Liberty huffed. "Well, of course I do!" Everyone gasped. "For goodness sakes," she said in exasperation. "I'm a private detective. I was called on the case by a good friend of Mr. Daniels. He wanted me to keep an eye open and see what I could find suspicious going on in this Chocolate Town. Since I'm from Philadelphia, no one knows me here. And the first thing I spotted when I got to Hershey was this peculiar family whose kids immediately tracked down the silver dollars the security guards were guarding. How do you explain that?!" She turned and glared at the children.

Now Mimi stepped forward, and Christina knew Miss Liberty was the one in big trouble. Mimi shook her red-polished fingernail (the color was OPI's Liar, Liar, Pants on Fire!) at Emmalou Liberty. "If someone calls these children nosy one more time," she warned, "they will have me to deal with!"

"Now, now," said Officer Chocolate gently. He stepped between the two women. He looked a little scared, as if things were getting out of his control. "Let's keep this civil, now."

Suddenly, there was a great hush as a little, old man in a wheelchair was wheeled into the room by a nurse. The man was wheeled right into the center of the crowd, then the nurse stepped back, folding her hands behind her back.

"Good evening," said the newcomer in a weak but pleasant voice. "My name is Mr. Daniels. I've been listening from the Circular

Dining Room. I understand everyone's concern and appreciate everyone's dismay over the recent events." With a kindly smile, he looked up at the four kids. "Especially these young children," he said, then added, "who paid me a visit earlier this evening."

Christina gasped. "But how did you know? We didn't see you. You didn't answer your door."

Grant couldn't contain himself. "But we saw your money!" he blurted. "About a gazillion silver dollars!"

Everyone gasped. "What?" asked Papa.

"What?" asked Mimi.

"Huh?" said Officer Chocolate.

"Do say?" said Miss Liberty.

"Are you sure?" Mr. Jasper asked the children. This time he sounded like he really cared about their opinion.

A slew of silver dollars!

22

MR. DANIEL'S SURPRISE!

Mr. Daniels' shoulders shook as he laughed softly. "Oh my, oh my," he said. "I didn't mean to cause such a stir. Such a ruckus. Sometimes it's so hard to do a nice thing. No one seems to expect it."

Christina came up and took the man's hand. He reminded her of her great-grandfather, Boom Pa, who was a World War II veteran, and who had died the previous year.

"We're so confused, sir," Christina said gently. "Could you explain this curious mystery to us? Please."

Once more, Mr. Daniels chuckled. "Oh, my goodness," he began. "It's like this. Mr. Hershey was so kind to me. I grew up in his home for boys...at that time, it was just for boys. Today, the Milton Hershey School serves about 1,500 children—boys and girls, from toddlers to college.

It's a wonderful thing. Just like Mr. Hershey and his beloved Kitty." For a moment, the old man looked like he might weep.

Then he went on. "I always saved part of my salary from the factory—I worked in Longitude, you know—in silver dollars. I wanted to make a donation to the school some day."

"Well, $900 is a nice donation," Christina said, giving the old man's hand a gentle squeeze.

"Nine hundred dollars?!" cried Mr. Daniels. "No, no, much more, young lady, much more."

"Do you mean $9,000 dollars?" asked Annabelle. That sounded like a lot of money.

Once more Mr. Daniels shook his balding head. "NO, NO!" he insisted. "MORE! MORE!"

For a moment, Christina feared that the old man was senile, or had Alzheimers disease, or something. She did not like the way he was getting so upset. She would not want him to have a heart attack, even if Mimi did carry an AED heart defibrillator with her at all times. "You just never know," she always said.

At the same time, the four children pictured the piles and stacks and walls and rooms of silver dollars that they had spotted through the window of Mr. Daniels' home. In a squeaky voice, Christina asked, "Surely you don't mean nine million dollars, do you?" she asked the old man.

Suddenly, Mr. Daniels beamed. "NINE MILLION! OF COURSE! NINE MILLION DOLLARS–ALL FOR THE MILTON HERSHEY SCHOOL! I want to give scholarships to students who want to go to college," he added.

Everyone began to laugh and applaud. But Mr. Daniels paid no attention. He just stared right into Christina's eyes. He stared harder and harder. He had a little grin on his face. And finally, he gave her a wink.

"OHHHHHHHHHHHHHHHH!" Christina finally squealed. "I understand!" she said.

The room got quiet again, except for some muttering in the back and a disturbance near the door.

Christina grinned back at the old man. "But someone tried to steal your money, didn't they?"

The old man nodded. The crowd drew closer.

"They thought they could just sneak it out a little at a time, right?" Christina went on. "Under false pretenses; is that right?"

Mr. Daniels nodded even harder.

"They just thought you were old and maybe not so smart anymore," Christina guessed. "Sorry, sir."

"Go on, girl!" Mr. Daniels insisted. He looked a little like a kid on Christmas morning knowing Santa has left gifts under the tree downstairs. "Knock 'em dead!"

Officer Chocolate stepped forward. "We'll have no talk like that, sir."

But Christina ignored everyone except Mr. Daniels and finished her story. "Someone wanted to 'help' protect Mr. Daniels' money," she told the crowd. "Like maybe offering to pick up some each day and take it to the bank vault for safekeeping?"

"And just who would that be?" Mr. Jasper asked, with a defensive tone in his voice.

Suddenly, the other kids caught on. All together, they pointed to the curly-headed woman trying desperately to sneak out of the room. "Stop, thief!" Grant cried, and the woman froze.

"A way-too-helpful bank teller!" said Christina.

"And now we've told on her!" said Annabelle.

Christina looked at Mr. Daniels to see if he was satisfied with her story. But he frowned and sliced his eyes sideways, rubbing his fingers together at the same time.

Suddenly Christina's "little gray cells," as she called them, got the message. Now she spoke loudly before the crowd dispersed. "BUT THE SILVER DOLLARS DIDN'T GO TO THE BANK VAULT. THE TELLER HAD HELP!" This time Christina did the pointing on her own. And it was toward the two so-called security guards.

Now, Papa got the full picture, too. "So you guys—what? The teller's brother? Boyfriend? You got the coins from her and disguised them until you could take them away and divvy them up. I suspect you were going to break in and get the rest of the silver dollars in that big moving truck parked out front? You varmints!"

"But what were the coins disguised like?" asked Sean.

Mimi laughed. "What everything around here wrapped in silver paper looks like, of course!"

All together, the four kids screamed: "CANDY!"

And Mr. Daniels, **jubilant**, laughed with glee!

130

23
HOT FUDGE SUNDAY!

The next morning, the *Hershey Chronicle* was headlined:

The Fountain Lobby of the Hotel Hershey was abuzz with folks ready to head for home.

Christina and Grant and their new friends said their goodbyes. They promised to be pen pals forever.

Mr. Daniels showed up and gave each kid a shiny silver dollar.

"You don't have to do that," Christina said. "This is for the school contribution. We don't mind making a donation. That's what we were coming to your house for."

"It's okay," said Mr. Daniels, as his nurse pushed his wheelchair down the corridor to a waiting car. "I saved these especially for special Hershey-kind-of-kids like you!"

"Boy, I can't wait to spend this!" said Grant.

Papa took the coin and looked at it. "This is a 1907 silver dollar, boy! You don't want to spend this—you need to save it!"

Grant groaned.

"Christina," Mimi said, "you did a great job of solving that curious mystery on the spot—especially with so few clues. But you kids sure gave me ideas for the plot of my Hershey mystery!"

"And is our reward to be in the book?" asked Annabelle, fingers crossed behind her back.

Mimi just smiled. She turned back to Christina and Sean, who were saying good-bye to one another a few feet away. "Christina, you never told me what you got at Hershey's Chocolate World," she said.

Sean grinned. "She got a Kiss!"

Mimi looked at her blushing granddaugther. "Is that right?" she asked.

Christina held out her hand filled with Hershey's Kisses. "Several," she said, honestly.

"You know what?" said Grant, tugging at his backpack while stopping to give a quick karate chop in the air.

"What?" they all asked.

"This Chocolate Town," said Grant, snitching one of his sister's Kisses, "really is the Sweetest Place on Earth!"

Well, that was fun!

Wow, glad we solved that mystery!

Where shall we go next?

EVERYWHERE!

The End

Now...go to

www.carolemarshmysteries.com

and...

- Add this book to your personal Adventure Map Tracker!

- Go on a Scavenger Hunt!

- Take a Pop(corn) Quiz!

- Hear from Mimi, Papa, Christina, and Grant!

- Talk to Christina and Grant!

- Join the Fan Club...and MUCH MORE!

Christina's Chocolate

Cacao beans
grow in pods.

The pods are cut open.

Sugar and milk are
mixed together
and extra water is
taken out.

COCOA
BUTTER

The milk/sugar mixture is added
to the cocoa butter. The paste
is conched and tempered.

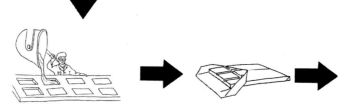

The chocolate is poured
into a mold.

Chocolate is wrapped to
keep it fresh.

-Making Scrapbook

Beans dry in the sun.

Bags of beans are
shipped to Hershey.

The beans are crushed into
a thin paste called chocolate liquor.
The liquor is pressed to separate
cocoa butter from cocoa solids.

The beans
are roasted.

The chocolate is shipped
to stores.

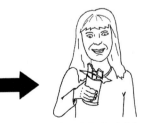

This chocolate is delicious!

The History of Chocolate

Chocolate has been around for a very long time. Here are some highlights in the sweet history of chocolate:

250-900 A.D.
The Mayan people in central Mexico ground cacao seeds into a paste. They mixed it with other ingredients like cornmeal, water, or chili peppers to make a spicy little concoction!

1200s
The Aztecs conquered the Mayans. They enjoyed chocolate, too! In fact, they Aztecs liked it so much that they began to use cacao beans as money. Chocolate was also used in religious ceremonies.

1500s
Spanish explorers in the New World were served chocolate drinks by the Aztecs. Explorer Hernando Cortez brought cacao beans and the recipe for the chocolate drink back to Europe. It was still a bitter brew, so the Spanish sweetened the drink with sugar. Mmmm...what a difference!

1600s

The demand for chocolate drinks spread across Europe. Chocolate was expensive, so only the wealthy could enjoy it. Plantations were established to grow cacao and sugar.

1700s

A machine was invented to grind cacao beans. A chocolate mill in the United States began to sell chocolate powder.

1800s

The first chocolate bar was created in England when cocoa powder, sugar, water, and melted cocoa butter were mixed and poured into molds. Creamy milk chocolate came about by adding condensed milk to melted chocolate. Machinery was invented during the Industrial Revolution to produce chocolate quickly and cheaply!

And the rest is HISTORY!

GLOSSARY

apprentice: a person who is learning a trade or craft by helping a skilled worker in that trade or craft

archives: collection of records and historical documents, or the place where such things are kept

confectioner: someone who makes candies or other sweets

consumption: the process of consuming or using up

conveyor: an endless belt used to carry things from one place to another in a factory

finagle: achieve something by means of trickery or devious methods.

philanthropist: someone who devotes time, money or efforts toward helping others; this term is usually applied to someone who gives large amounts of money to charity

skeptical: having or showing doubt; not believing easily

union: a group of workers joined together to promote and protect their interests

SAT GLOSSARY

entrepreneur: a person who takes the risk of starting a new business

excursion: a short trip taken for pleasure

jubilant: joyful and proud; glad

opulent: deluxe; rich and superior in quality

rancid: bad odor or smell coming from a spoiled oily product

Enjoy this exciting excerpt from:

THE MYSTERY AT

Disney World

WE'RE GOING TO DISNEY WORLD!

"I'm going to Disneyland!" shouted Grant, jumping up and down on Christina's bed. This wasn't her brother's first trip to Disney, but he sure acted like it, his sister Christina thought.

"Grant!" she cried. "It's 5 a.m.! Go back to sleep. The park doesn't open for another four hours!" When Grant didn't stop bouncing up and down, Christina threw her pillow at Grant and knocked him down. "Go back to bed!"

Grant hopped off of Christina's bed, stuck his tongue out at his sister, and headed straight for Mimi and Papa's room in their condominium. He didn't care if the park didn't open for another 24 hours, he wanted to be first in line. Much to Grant's surprise, Papa was sitting at the table in the kitchen reading the morning paper.

"Good morning, kiddo!" Papa said, as he sipped his cup of coffee.

"I'm going to Disneyland!" shouted Grant again.

Papa laughed and said, "Actually, you are going to Disney World. Disneyland is in Anaheim, California, and we are in Orlando, Florida."

"Oh," Grant said. "I'm going to Disney World!"

Papa just smiled and went back to reading his Orlando Sentinel. Christina came out of the bedroom stretching and yawning. She was just as excited about being in Orlando as Grant was. When Mimi and Papa invited Grant and Christina to go to Disney World, Christina could hardly wait. She knew that Mimi had never been to Disney World. And since Christina had been many times before—Papa called her a seasoned pro—she planned to show Mimi the ropes!

"Morning, Papa," she said, as she headed into the kitchen. Grabbing her favorite cereal, a carton of milk, and two bowls and spoons, Christina joined Grant and Papa at the table. She knew that between writing a mystery and visiting Disney World, Mimi was going to have a busy day, so she fixed breakfast for herself and Grant while Mimi slept in.

"Morning, princess," Papa said, as he finished his paper. Papa woke up early every morning—even when they were on vacation—to walk a few miles, and read the morning paper. "How did you sleep?"

"I couldn't go to sleep!" interrupted Grant. "I didn't sleep a wink!"

"Oh, and I suppose that's why you woke me up five times with your snoring last night," Christina teased.

"Did not!" Grant protested.

"Did too!" Christina shrieked.

"Did not!" Grant shouted again.

"All right, all right you two!" Papa said, as he finished his cup of coffee. "Grant, why don't you go get the map of the park, so we can plot our adventure for today!"

Papa always knew how to stop Christina and Grant from arguing.

Grant quickly ran into their bedroom to get the Magic Kingdom map that the people at Disney had sent to Mimi for her book research. Christina cleared their cereal bowls and Papa's coffee cup, and put them into the dishwasher.

When she returned to the table, Papa had already spread out the colorful map for them all to see.

"So, Christina, where do you want to go first?" Papa asked.

With no hesitation at all, Christina answered, "Tomorrowland! Space Mountain is my favorite roller coaster ever!"

"Well, I want to go to Frontierland!" insisted Grant. "Big Mountain Railroad Thunder is my favorite roller coaster ever!"

"Grant! It's the Big Thunder Mountain Railroad, silly." Christina laughed.

"That's what I said, Christina. The Big Mountain Railroad Thunder."

This time, Christina didn't even attempt to correct him.

"And look," Grant boasted. "I even brought my coonskin cap that I got in San Antonio at the Alamo." Grant grinned as he put the hat on backwards so that the tail went right down the middle of his face.

"Oh, Grant! You are so silly!" Christina giggled.

"Well kids, we have all day, so don't worry, we'll make it to both attractions," Mimi said, as she joined them at the table.

"I'm sorry Mimi! Did we wake you up?" Christina said. "I told Grant not to be so loud."

"Oh, it's alright. We have a lot of planning to do and I want to be a part of it!"

Mimi always woke up in a great mood, Christina thought. Unlike Mimi, Christina didn't like getting up in the morning, especially when Grant would jump on her bed and scream at the top of his lungs. Being a human alarm clock was his favorite way to wake his sleeping sister.

"Alright, so let's make a plan!" Mimi said, her pad and pencil in hand. Christina didn't remember ever seeing her grandmother without something to write on. Usually, it was her laptop computer. But, she decided lugging a laptop around the nearly 30,000 acres of Disney World didn't sound like too much fun, so she opted for the old-fashioned way—pencil and paper.

"There are six lands in Disney World: Adventureland, Frontierland, Fantasyland, Tomorrowland, Mickey's Toontown Fair, and Liberty Square," said Mimi.

"Mickey's Toontown Fair and Liberty Square aren't lands, Mimi!" Grant laughed. He loved when he knew something the adults didn't. "Well, although they don't have land in their names, that's what Walt Disney called them," Mimi corrected.

"But first you have to go through Main Street, U.S.A," stated Christina very matter-of-factly.

"Very good, Christina," Papa said. Although he liked to help plan their trips, Christina knew that whatever Mimi wanted to do was what Papa wanted to do. "So where to first?"

"I know, I know!" Grant said, squirming in his seat. "Frontierland!"

"Well, I have an idea," said Mimi. "Why don't we go clockwise? We'll start here at Adventureland," she said as she pointed to the map, "and we'll work our way all the way around to Tomorrowland."

Christina knew that Mimi was being diplomatic. If she went counterclockwise, they would start with Christina's favorite—Tomorrowland, and Grant wouldn't be very happy about that. With Mimi's plan, they wouldn't start with anyone's favorite. And secretly she hoped that Grant would be so tired by the time they made it to Tomorrowland that he wouldn't want to ride Space Mountain with her.

"Sounds great to me!" said Grant.

"Sounds wonderful to me!" Papa agreed.

"Sounds perfect to me!" Christina said, with a laugh.

"Then we are agreed!" Mimi smiled.

All of a sudden Mimi jumped up from the table with a panicked look on her face and said, "Oh my goodness!"

"What's the matter, Mimi?" Christina said worriedly. "Did you forget something?"

"Oh, no!" Mimi gasped.

"What, what?" Grant insisted.

"Just look at the clock!" Mimi cried.

Enjoy this exciting excerpt from:

THE MYSTERY AT Big Ben

GETTING THERE IS HALF THE FUN!

"*BONG! BONG!*" cried Grant. "*BONG... BONG... BONG... BONG!*"

"Grant, if you *bong* one more time, I'm going to *bong* you on the head," his grandmother Mimi said.

They were standing in the middle of busy Heathrow Airport watching for Papa and Grant's sister Christina to appear with the luggage. They had just flown in from Paris aboard Papa's little red and white airplane, *The Mystery Girl.*

Suddenly, an overflowing luggage cart appeared. It staggered left and right toward them as if propelled by a seasick ghost.

Grant jumped just before the cart ran over his foot. "Hey, careful there!" he screeched.

A head thrust out from each side of the cart. "I can't believe we have so much luggage," Papa said. He looked handsome in the cowboy hat and boots and leather vest he always wore, but he was panting like a dog.

Christina plopped down on the floor. "This luggage cart is crazy. I thought we'd never get this stuff pushed all the way over here. I'm exhausted!"

"*BONG! BONG! BONG!*" cried Grant yet again.

Christina and Papa stared at him like he was crazy. "And just what is that all about?" Papa asked, holding his head with both hands.

Mimi sighed. "Grant thinks he will just die if we don't go see Big Ben right away," she explained. "I do not know why he is so excited about a clock."

Grant thrust his hands on his hips in his don't-make-fun-of-me-just-cause-I'm-only-seven pose. "It isn't just any old clock," he said. "Big Ben is the most famous clock in the world. It's tall and it's loud and I want to see it."

"I doubt that it's as loud as you," Christina teased her brother. She brushed her bangs away from her forehead.

"I doubt anything's as loud as Grant," Papa agreed.

"He's loud, but he's cute and sweet," Mimi said, tousling Grant's blond crewcut, "but I'm still going to *bong* him on the head if he imitates Big Ben anymore till we go and see it for ourselves."

"*Bong...bong...*" whispered Grant.

"What's that?" Christina asked.

"LITTLE BEN!" Grant cried and laughed.

Papa ended the discussion by saying, "Here, pard'ner!" and dumping a large duffle bag into Grant's arms.

"*Ufgh!*" said Grant, swaying under the weight. He wandered left and right. All you could see was the bag and his little arms holding on for dear life and his legs quivering beneath him.

Christina laughed until Papa said, "You, too, Missy!" and tossed her a suitcase that seemed to weigh a ton.

"These are too heavy!" Christina complained.

"Then next time don't pack so much," said Papa. "Those are *your* bags, you know." Papa threw a hanging bag over his shoulder and picked up a small case. "And these are mine," he said with a smile.

Grant had dropped his duffle to the floor.

Christina did the same. "Then whose are all those?!" they asked, pointing to a large mound of bright red suitcases of all sizes.

Papa looked at Mimi. Christina looked at Mimi. Grant looked at Mimi. Mimi looked at the ceiling, ignoring them all.

"Mimi!" Christina squealed. "What is all that stuff?"

Mimi looked at them and smiled secretively. "Oh, you know. This and that. I do have to meet the Queen, you know. And I have to write a mystery, you know. So, you know, I need a lot of stuff."

Papa just shook his head tiredly. Christina and Grant laughed. Mimi wrote mystery books for kids and set them in real locations, like the one she would be working on here in London, England. Papa was "travel agent" and "trail boss." And when Christina and Grant were out of school, they got to tag along, and were supposed to stay out of the way... but they never did! Why? Because they felt it was their official job to help Mimi discover mysterious facts and places and people to put in her books.

But sometimes, things backfired. Like now? For suddenly, there was a loud BOOM which echoed throughout the busy terminal.

"What was that?" said Mimi.

"Was it a bomb?" Christina asked. She knew there had been some terrorist bombs in London in the past.

"No!" said Grant. "It's that!"

They all turned around and stared at the overloaded luggage cart which had tipped and fallen over, tossing all of Mimi's red luggage to the floor.

"*Ufgh!*" said Papa with a sigh and began to hoist all the suitcases back into place.